Lynn Saville

About the Author

SABRA LOOMIS is the author of *Rosetree*, published by Alice James Books, and of two chapbooks of poetry. She divides her time between New York City and Achill Island, County Mayo. She has received awards from the Massachusetts Artists Foundation, the Yeats Society, and the British Council. For two years she was curator of Camilla's, a reading series in New York associated with Circle in the Square Theatre. She teaches frequently at the Joiner Center, University of Massachusetts, Boston, and was on the faculty of the Poets' House, Donegal, for many years.

ALSO BY SABRA LOOMIS

Rosetree
The Blue Door
The Ship

The National Poetry Series was established in 1978 to ensure the publication of five poetry books annually through participating publishers. Publication is funded by the Lannan Foundation; the late James A. Michener and Edward J. Piszek through the Copernicus Society of America; Stephen Graham; International Institute of Modern Letters; Joyce and Seward Johnson Foundation; Juliet Lea Hillman Simonds Foundation; and the Tiny Tiger Foundation. This project also is supported in part by an award from the National Endowment for the Arts, which believes that a great nation deserves great art.

2006 Open Competition Winners

Joe Bonomo of DeKalb, Illinois, *Installations*
Chosen by Naomi Shihab Nye, to be published by Penguin Books

Oni Buchanan of Brighton, Massachusetts, *Spring*
Chosen by Mark Doty, to be published by University of Illinois Press

Sabra Loomis of New York, New York, *House Held Together by Winds*
Chosen by James Tate, to be published by Harper Perennial

Donna Stonecipher of Seattle, Washington, *The Cosmopolitan*
Chosen by John Yau, to be published by Coffee House Press

Rodrigo Toscano of Brooklyn, New York, *Collapsible Poetics Theater*
Chosen by Marjorie Welish, to be published by Fence Books

HOUSE
HELD TOGETHER
BY WINDS

SABRA LOOMIS

HARPER  PERENNIAL

NEW YORK • LONDON • TORONTO • SYDNEY • NEW DELHI • AUCKLAND

HARPER ● PERENNIAL

NATIONAL
ENDOWMENT
FOR THE ARTS

HarperCollins books may be purchased for educational, business, or sales promotional use. For information please write: Special Markets Department, HarperCollins Publishers, 10 East 53rd Street, New York, NY 10022.

FIRST EDITION

Designed by Justin Dodd

Library of Congress Cataloging-in-Publication Data
Loomis, Sabra.
    House held together by winds / Sabra Loomis.—1st Harper Perennial ed.
        p.   cm.

ISBN 978-0-06-157715-4

08 09 10 11 12 ID/RRD 10 9 8 7 6 5 4 3 2 1

To my brother and sisters

Contents

Acknowledgments

Grateful acknowledgment is made to the following journals and anthologies for poems that appeared in them, sometimes in slightly different form:

The American Poetry Review: "Echo" and "Woman and Donkey"; *Cyphers*: "Bring the Lambs," "Elephant," "Geography Lesson," "Like Music," and "The Bear He Shot on Their Honeymoon in Montana, That Growled, and Tried to Come into Their Tent," and "War Stories"; *Heliotrope*: "The Blue Door" and "Tunnels"; *St. Ann's Review*: "It Was Time"; *Poetry Ireland Review*: "Learning the Game of Go," "The Alphabet of Singing," and "Hearing the Voices"; *Poetry New York*: "The Trouble I Have in High Places" and "Two Daughters He Let Fall"; *Salamander*: "Delia," "In Mary Hoban's Garden," "In the Mountains," "The Music Cabinet," and "To My Achill Neighbors in the Wind and Rain"; *The Recorder*: "Letter from Achill," "Aphrodite," "Traveling on Blue," "Small Goats," and "Along the Quarry Road."

"ESP" won honorable mention in the Lumina Poetry competition and was published in *Lumina*.

"Fur Coats" and "The Ship" won awards in the Short Grain Writing Contest and were published in *Grain*.

"Parachutes" was runner-up for the Oberon Poetry Prize, and appeared in *Oberon*.

"The Alphabet of Singing" won the Yeats Society Annual Poetry Competition and was published in *Poetry Ireland Review.*

Poems have appeared in many anthologies, including *The American Voice Anthology*; *The Book of Irish-American Poetry: From the 18th Century to the Present*, from Notre Dame Press; *Four Way Reader #2*; *Present Tense: Poems and Photographs from County Mayo*; and *Salamander: Then and Now 10th Anniversary*.

LEARNING THE GAME OF GO

Fur Coats

There may have been a jaguar. Or a leopard found its way in, from ancient parties on the lawn. A panther found its way through locked doors, carried the weathered calm of its skin upstairs, past mirrored landings, the Venetian glass figurines staring with white hands into the dark. The glass monkey with milk-white hat danced and held his hat up for a penny. The black panther stood and rubbed his pelt against the dining room table, blew through his nostrils with a Whiff! into the dark. Wind was the way he came in; wind blew the French doors in the dining room open. He followed his own rhythm upstairs, in the reflections on mirrored walls. In the dressing room, a quilted mirror rose on a long stem from the dark. There may have been boxes of pins, of old hatpins and opinions. The panther could get in by the temptation things had among themselves to remain silent. He hid his agate eyes among the garments, where there was a handbag with a fierce gold clasp. The way things had, that were lost or stolen, of turning up again at night. The way things that were watched had, of turning their faces to the wall. The panther glided in behind mirrors, where he could hide among black satin shoes. He disappeared, into the black backing of the mirrors.

ESP

Her uncle was very clear.
She had to stand in the other room
while he guessed her thoughts,
the numbers she was thinking.

They were in a cavern,
a canyon by the stairs.
She didn't like the fact
he could read her thoughts.

Before the war, he was a mountain climber.
She listened as new mountains were discovered
and climbed: Nanda Devi, Annapurna, Everest.

They drew close to the mountains
in sleep. And a strange singing
came from the high-up houses.
The house itself was a landscape:
messages carved in the corners.

On this plateau,
what were the signs of life?
Herons and crows, magpies
with black-and-white markings.

She was his new experiment.
Mountains piled up
with energy in the layers—
the brain as a new Himalaya.

When news came from the front,
when the snows melted,
they took off the tough hide shoes,
stood at the windows and listened.

She started to guess
what he might be thinking.
Separation: a narrow rope bridge
across a chasm. You went on your knees
if at all, he said, out over the brink.

What markings were there in the cloud landscape?
Who were the singers?
Where was the precipice?

It Was Time

In her grandmother's house
you went in through a hallway,
with a lantern
beside the heavy front door.

The hallway
filled with books of the imagination:
words rocked by winds:
Treasure Island, Two Years Before the Mast.

Where light fell
through borders
of a stained glass window.

If you went up through time,
through this hallway, you trusted
to the one dim lamp—
for details noticed in childhood:
more, as years went on.

It was Time.
Her uncle was traveling
up a steep, winding path
that started from the foot of Tower Hill.

The uncle, grandmother, and child
were all traveling together—
with tales of chivalry: *Tristan and Isolde,
Héloise and Abelard.*

Stories filled them,
lifted them higher.
In the house with casement windows,
a terrace, and a loveseat.

Titles of novels breathed at them
from the spines of books:
the halls with clear echoes,
easy lies—
about the bravery in battle.

The uncle traveled
with Chinamen,
the Five Immortals,
along the corridors of wintry light,
where they were snowbound each morning.

It was the grandmother's time
they were reading, and recording.

It was *Le Livre du Coeur d'Amour Épris.*
Young King René lived there.
He put on white armor
with the sacred, red heart

and journeyed into the world.
It was Time. You try not to forget too much.

He took off his hat, his helmet,
and dreamed beside a well.
Through the world at midnight
the moon guided him. There was a small chapel.
A house with high-pitched roof and a side porch—

and a light that stayed on,
from an earlier generation.

Parachutes

How many grown-ups there were then, dressing the children in velvet. In trousers with loops underfoot, and the children wanted to stay up late, meet the admiral who was coming to dinner. To hang over the landing from above, see the stately old cousin arrive in a greatcoat. They longed to be grown-up: considered expert on shoes or wedding gifts or party invitations.

Here came the grown-ups, the uncles with watch-chain and vest.

All dressed up again, it was endless. Their shoes sat on wooden trees, their umbrellas had circus animals carved on the handles, out of wood or tortoiseshell. Her uncle's friends sat very straight in the hallway downstairs, waiting to be announced. Their hands rested on the umbrella handles. Those fathers and uncles who jumped out of airplanes, who joined the OSS to bail out over China and Burma. They would shout—and the parachutes opened. They floated down out of the dark like dandelion seeds, each with his own parachute. And did they shoot anyone? No one was saying anymore. No one ever said.

WAR STORIES

How the Chinese laughed
when they saw people killed on the runway—
rolled flat by an airstrip roller.

That was her uncle,
telling his war-headed tales.

Her grandmother rested.
Birds landed around her
from bedposts, limbs
of the dining room wallpaper.

Did she have friends in the beehive?
Did she expect the mirrors to talk?

Listening to birds kept her occupied
in her tall white bedroom at the top of the stairs.
Delia and Mary tiptoed and learned to listen.
Delia knocked at the door, turned down the bed.

The chimneys stored
the dust of mirrors.
Halos for bravery
hung along walls,
on heads of the angels
in her grandmother's bedroom.

As for the child, her uncle
kept her awake in the night
telling war stories. He was resting
from the war in the Pacific. He was "On leave."

The paratroopers flew like birds
to a cave near the Pacific.
They learned to jump 200 feet
to the ocean, without killing themselves.
Perfectly straight, her uncle said—
so they didn't break their necks.

His eyes went into straight lines
at the corners, from squinting across mountains,
snowfields. His eyes were a sunlit struggle.

Much later, they were in a theater together,
the child, her mother, and the uncle:
for a film called *Flying Tigers*.
Her mother wanted her to see the danger:
how pilots were smashed against windscreens,
fell from the half-open cockpits.
She cried to get out of the theater,
onto the pavements and the wet, shining grass.

Learning the Game of Go

In the living room their stepfather taught them
the Japanese game of Go,
used to train officers of the Japanese army.
Was war then a game,
like Blindman's Bluff
or Capture the Flag?

She was six, in the living room
when he gave her as handicap
a quarter of the Go board.

To jump, or parachute in
and surround the enemy.
It could have been a jungle
or a mountain fastness.
It could have been the place
his younger brother Farnie
took the paratroop training,
learning to jump into the mountains of China.

To hide in a riverbed,
moving horses up
through corridors between mountains.
Some, like his brother, were waiting
for the weather to change. So they could bring
horses across the bright, high passes
from Mongolia to China.

She was six
when her stepfather gave her
a quarter of the Go board.
When he gave her the icy corridors,
to think fast and plan ahead,
in wartime.

Some like his brother
were waiting for the weather to change.
So they could see out
through the mist over mountains,
find houses and bread
and rest for the horses.

How to penetrate blue mountain caverns
with horses, with supplies for Chiang Kai-shek.

They learned to dissemble
and hide their intentions. How to retreat,
before the enemy could guess your position.
How to create a diversion—
in some other part of the world or house—
some other "front" of the Go board.

THE GRANDFATHER

1.
He built high-tension wires
across the country, and amassed a fortune.
It was highly tense
to live with him, you had to answer
all his questions at dinner.

The children had to answer questions
about flies taking off
and landing on railroad trains.

He measured the electricity of the brain,
invented the loran system of navigation.

He could play tricks,
card tricks—you never saw the cards move.

Close by, in the laboratory or glass house
where they were forbidden to go—
there was a busy world. There were experiments.
There was a key, there were always keys
to hidden rooms. The games went on.

Rum cocktails mixed by Delia in the kitchen,
arriving on a little tray.

There may have been rough places, cracks
in a window, or the servants' wing.
Some actual tears in fact, who knew?

He was a friend to everyone:
Niels Bohr and the atomic physicists;
the Secretary of War.

Up in his laboratory measuring brain waves,
running away with the lab assistant's wife.

2.
What happens if a fly
tries to land on a railroad train
and the train is moving?
(it was always moving night and day)

They had to celebrate their birthdays
in the morning. Busy the rest of the day,
he helped blow out the birthday candles
at breakfast. It was Greenwich Mean Time.

They were flying out to sea,
testing the new radar. On the crests of waves,
the crest of the times. It was an adventure.
They were out of sight of land most of the time.

Anticipating the Stock Market Crash,
he had removed all his money to Switzerland.

What if it rained that morning?
You had to know how fast the train was going—
What if a wind blew in from the dead?

3.
They had to answer his questions
about flies landing on railroad trains.

What happens if the fly is happy,
trusting the earth?
First it's small and still,
then moves closer. Then, thinking it over,
it moves away again. What happens if cracks appear
in the chill air around you, when you are a hero?

House Held Together by Winds

From perches high
under the roof
children looked down, as footsteps
went underneath the boughs.

It was feasting,
as if climbing an apple tree.

They were brought in by the nurse to visit
dressed in red velvet dresses
sometimes a lace collar.

In winter black seeds
fell into the ground
through holes
where the wind and snow had crept in.

The grandmother was seated
next to the fireplace, reading her book.
Between firewood and fire screen—and the bellows.
They were brought in to visit her
about the time the snow and wind
blew around the house's holly.
Horses stamped in their stalls,
in new stables.

Snow layered the wind.
The lamps and the bellows were bright.
They were brought to visit her
about the time the Snow Leopard of wind
blew round the house, rattling the dead holly leaves.

A little god spoke out of the fire.
She had to use all her powers against him
when winter's storms began,
the clouds lifted high above their heads.

Drafts came,
shaking the fringes of curtains.
The fire tried to leap out
from the place where the grandmother was sitting.

They spoke little,
as firelight made shadows on the wall.
She had to rise often
to put another log on the fire,
or stir up the embers
and they saw many things:
fire children rising and swimming away
like the Water Babies—or the face of a fox.

She held the keys to her own place,
and she was not too delicate.

She bided her time in the storms,
as winter came and went.

In the Mountains

THE SHIP

When they had climbed up the high pine hill, they saw a cloud rapidly approaching. As it flew near and skirted around them, they saw it was a ship. It was drawing streamers, hundreds of colorful streamers after it; like a bird coming to rest on a hilltop, or a rainbow breathing the air. Down it came, the shrouds and halyards rattling, and they held to the gunwales and climbed aboard. As the ship moved away from land, they saw farther than they had ever seen before. The skies were every shade of blue, until far out on the horizon. They held tight to the gunwales, which were also of blue, and along with the exploring, the hunger of waves, came a calm deeper than they had known. *Come shrouds, come flowering of a shipboard hunger* . . . Drawing near the sun, they were themselves again, with the great salt stars, tasting of grief. They saw the girth, the far edges of childhood, and labored to draw in the sky like a sail. They held on into the blue, in spite of words and a murmur of voices, and night, and the turning of the waves.

WOMAN AND DONKEY

The donkey refuses
to carry these rocks any farther.
On the saddle of land between Slievemore
and Dooagh, with a hee-haw he stops.
Then up again, with wooden climbing
under clouds up a stairway of rocks.

She wants to open the mountain
and plunge in, to tear apart
fields, wade in among the clouds.
She wants to tear apart the white grammar of clouds.

The cattle lie like buttresses
along a hillside. She has her wall of echoes,
protected: back from the road behind a gate.

She has her chill walk of echoes,
going with firm step
up a side path, through weeds and nettles.

She wants to open the still-dying gates of the fields
to the blue gentian of a mountain;
with low-bursting clouds, clouds flying—
wants to open the water fields to the fringes of death.

Her donkey sits down.
He has his wall of pebbles,
his plate of time for changes.
The donkey sits. His plate is full,
tossed with white crumbs: the lonely clouds.

In the Mountains

Who builds the strong
movements of water downward
stealing through the grass?

The mountains
gather the confidence of the sunrise
into their palms and on their cheekbones,
the punctilious, blue eyes of flowers in the grass.

They gather undercurrents,
leaping movements of streams:

to build the terraced sunrise outward,
and to let clouds rise and settle
on their chins and shoulder blades.

Where it meets the bank,
the stream is bright
with small water-plants,
bowing to and fro across the current.

Into the hills'
great rhythmical shells
they move, to get inside sunlight,
to bring us the music of steps, and of stones.

THE ALPHABET OF SINGING
for Achill Island

I wanted to pronounce
and keep the alphabets alive.
My birds and lambs were the letters,
lambs standing beside their mothers,
pushing against the mothers' ribs
in the alphabet of singing.

The birds I was feeding
flocked away, and grew hungrier.
They robbed me—it didn't matter.

I was keeper of the dark green alphabet of woods,
a keeper of sounds, and of arrows. My green sounds
were words like "moon" and "hunting dog" and "sheep,"
hungry words like "lodging" and "apples."

I pressed *down* with my larynx,
my tongue arched dark
to keep syllables rounded,
the notes and letters moving and alive:

green insect words like "mantis" or "mayfly,"
"house" or "windows" or "caring."

My birds took flight and curved
to the horizon. They grew hungrier
by daylight. Sounds within my ribs,
casting to left and right,
like a sower in fields
moving his shadow across the furrows.

At night, in my hut on the mountainside,
I was keeper of words, and the ordinary daylight sounds:
dogs barking, or the clanging shut of a gate.

At night, when I lay down to sleep at the foot of the village,
the apples rolled away from me, down a steep hill in the
    falling light;
the apples rolled silently, intently, down a green hill.

HERMIT

He needs to be fenced in. Week after week, he needs the solace of winds, and of the animals. And to grow flowers, in the warm sun.

Down the road they've been watching him from high dormer windows. He needs to keep things moving, like the red fox who comes through the garden at evening, through a hole in the backyard fence. Who comes and stands near the flax bushes. The fence widens out, into those caves and hollow rooms he slept in as a child. Slept sometimes outside, under big oaks. He doesn't know why the fox comes at twilight, watching for him. While others pass by, outside and around. He must mend the broken fence. He begins to feel a pressure outward, begins to mold it as an artist would: like the red fox traveling dry, sanded paths. He also feels a separation. The pleasure of standing still, letting the world pass by around and outside him.

SMALL GOATS

White goats
listening at the edges
of the barn, or higher up
along grass-green ledges
of a hillside, beside a stream.

When they saw me coming they came back,
placed their forefeet on the wooden crossbars
of the gate. They listened attentively
from the shadow of tree trunks,
or from deeper shadows, inside the barn.

Touching the animal light of their existences,
in waves of sleep at the crown of the head;
touching the crown, to feel its height,
the beginning of horns, as I reached my hand
through the wooden crossbars.

They are a gift. They are half in and out
of the shadows. I wanted the line of their silvery heads,
feeling the narrowness of two eyes
and to touch, to enter the legato
of the forehead and two horns.

Walking in from some distant part
of the farm, and herded away from wind,
they were gathered there, by the corral fence.

What I wanted was to feel a kernel
of their presence, the animal peace.

Touching the light tulip-fur
of the forehead, with fine news.
Keeping the gossip of the hills
alive and coming to me over crossbars,
watching through narrowed spaces of the corral gate.

IN MARY HOBAN'S GARDEN

Here she is alone,
in the wind books of the iris.

Walking silently,
on a path that turns around
to the side of the house:
keeping brambles and thorns
away from bleeding hearts.

The cat lies down on the walk
in front of the house. From under eyelids
he sees clouds, bushes. The day is overcast.
He lies sideways in the grass,
on this side, or the other, of the path.

Round, ruffled wind-sounds
of the peonies by the front gate:
by a glassed-in porch
that serves as a windbreak
for the cat lying there quietly.

She fishes down through cloud-layers
to reach him—through a striped,
pale cover of iris leaves.
She wants to lift him—he wants to leap,
to lie full-length in the grass again.

She closes out the clouds,
leaning above. She is the guardian
of the cat, and the birds at the bird feeder.
He sees this, from shining, grey eyes,
from under eyelids. This is the path.

She'll move away soon
and re-enter the house,
fastening behind her the wooden door.

Outside, the tiger lilies walk away.
They follow the habit of going down over bridges,
to a café, by the harbor.
The tiger lilies walk down the road to the hotel.
They love the hedges, heavy with rain,
and the clean scent of bridges.

Aphrodite

Along the brink you come,
       waiting for ornaments of the tide.
With amulets of sea shells
picking their way up, breathing between the layers.

With sounds of an iron ring,
a curragh scraping against a seawall.

Travel,
to release the light sounds of oarlocks.

Scavenge, and fasten threads to a garden wall.

How to carry the rose garden of your life
       higher, above a shoreline.

It has always been there, teasing thought
with the idea of becoming green again.

How to carry the garden free of old iris petals.
    Spade, shifting the dirt from winter winds.

Travel all the way up to the garden
for a light, after-dinner walk.

    Ramble through a rose-tide.

Come in,
over the garden's east wall,
    with a new way of walking, of releasing sounds.

With blue-green fishnets, thinking about the fishnets.

Some of these have come a long way
        with knotted, free lines—
weaving definite webs for the shoreline hours.

Drag hard against the seawalls.
Come from beneath, with your talking, with your breath.

TRAVELING ON BLUE

THE BLUE DOOR

Leonard the gardener had a wheelbarrow full of gold, when they were children. As he wheeled it down the road, the fields hid voices. Bits of wool were sticking to the fence posts, the rivers. The children had their sand-castles, and sunhouses. As he wheeled his blue hope of a house along the road, the sun went behind a cloud. The children hid their sunhouses, behind a fence. The children were the mad gardener Leonard, who thought the woods were full of gold. As he wheeled his blue heron, his house down the road, the sun was sinking. The heron dived into the sun.

A tractor comes downhill, trailing a blue plume of smoke. Across the valley, on the opposite hillside, mountains are walking high in the air. Don't go near, I said to my house, my garden. A mountain lion lives near here. Stones were the grey steps, leading down. The mountain lion came into the garden. Birds stayed awake, in the steep, sunlit air.

ECHO

He forced their mother, many years ago,
to submit to the honeymoon conditions.
She had to climb mountains in the daytime,
he held her over a cliff—

he dangled her,
making her swear she wasn't frightened,
that she was a woman and she trusted him.

If she combed her long, honey-blonde hair,
she had to climb the high mountains with him,
be dangled over cliffs—
with a Valentine waistline and heavy-lidded eyes.

(she must despise him now)
No, she must depend on him now,
like a voice and its echo.

She trusted him night and morning
and had managed to walk
across the high, narrow footbridge of his life
away from the grief, and the utterance
of her own life.

And so,
so,
she must depend on him now.

Etruscan

Rain is coming,
bringing cattle
home through hedges at nightfall.

Hurry to the gate—
to look beyond, to see beyond
ourselves: through a web of roots
uphill, through a gap in the willows.

Wild waters beyond childhood
breathe into the dusk.
They are carried like weight into tree bark,
and the listening hide of trees.

Forage for the spells
that lie underneath a gate.

Bringing cattle to the edges of fields;
to push their heads forward
and drink beneath the wires.

They breathe in the dusk
behind a field gate.
With wide, Etruscan eyes
and a ragged breath, at nightfall.

Tunnels

There is room now, running downwind;
new urge, new current rising
from the heaped-up earth of tunnels.

Breaking like fire from the hill
then sighing, giving way
in thorn trunks, the hazel trees.

There's room under the hill
for the brown fox and her kits.
Rooms widen out, listening—
then melt away.

Breathing like fire from the hill;
and looking away from the hill.

Will you build a house
to melt
downwind over green slopes,
with apples on the ground?

Here's my new address:
mother, wind, bird, salient.

Lying in a field of stone,
among thorns. Note the nourishment.

Two Daughters He Let Fall

He let his child, the infant
slip away from him
in the breath of stillness
on the evening terrace.

On the ocean of the terrace
they came onto the milk-white balconies
and never said a word.

He let the child slip from his arms,
let the cocoon of the child
drift down away from him
then buried his head in his arms
and never said a word.

On the ocean of the terrace
where ships meet far out in the distance;
where once a whale was stranded.

Did she die?
She didn't die.

He let the second daughter
slip away from them in the snow-white boat,
falling into a wake of shadows.
Far below them she drifted, in a cauldron of dreams.

Evening was disappearing;
coming up, disappearing.

Behind her,
the whalebone beach was deserted.

She came up breathing fire-water;
full of brown seaweed and discords,
notes and signals from the ocean's depths.

The bumping of a dinghy
when he tossed her back onboard—
as if on dry land—back
into her childhood.

Traveling on Blue

Under the stars of bending
I took in the lowing of herds,
tasted and received
the waters of their hides
wandering over bog myrtle.

I stepped carefully,
in waters of the blue-black herds.
The great heads nodded and revolved
to see me as I walked.

Fragrance of holly, and I held still:
let primroses, let clover fall
over the arched neck, over nape and horns.
I held these gifts as an offering,
carved by the hooves and still horns of the cattle.

The tongue of tidewater reflected me
as it climbed over banks.
In late evening advancing,
through the nettle farms and islands of blue sky,
islands of the blue sea holly.

LETTER FROM ACHILL

A circular hollow occurs,
carved with whatever creatures
came this way in the night,
pressing down corridors of sleep
between the houses.

A doorway surrounded by flames,
set into a green hill.
Planted with white daisies
that grew along the Dugort shore.

Joe the handyman watches swans
through the binoculars. There were 200 pairs
on the lake in earlier years,
before the windsurfers
frightened them away.

Windsurfers
sign their names outside the reeds
at the end of the shore road.
They trouble the quick brown water
with their cries, while the handyman watches.

Deep in the woods
my initial is carved;
in a hollow filled with ferns
and knotted up with vines.
A staircase of the wind flows into it.

The Trouble I Have in High Places

ZIFFY-STERNAL

When the stepfather made a motion
of guiding his knuckles in their direction,
the children ran to hide
behind the living room sofa.

But he reached in after them,
like God reaching after Adam in the depths of Time,
because he needed the strength
that came to him from child-flesh,
sinking his knuckles in the quick-breathing bodies.

He'd grind his knuckles
into their waists,
called it a "ziffy-sternal."

He needed to touch the children with whatever fear was,
bring his knuckles into the silence again.
He pushed through the blue-eyed fear of the child,
out the other side—like going through a field
of new wheat or barley—into what light of a new world?

The children understood
their wilderness had been trampled on,
their childhood home left far behind
(at the meeting of two rivers), and they would never
in this world ever again reach home,
or the kindliness, the equal handling they had known
    before.

SHAME

Is it petty to extract these tales?

She could be the child
of a laughing prince.
She could be fallen down behind the sofa—
fallen down, lost, *wedged*—child of a
(drunken) far-off prince.
Take this child, run away with her . . .

On the staircase elevator
she rides down into secrets,
the scent of jasmine and potpourri.

She could be stepdaughter
to a pirate. Laughing (as he is too).
Snobbish. Pretending to be kind.

Give her the run of the house.
She runs on, in front of mirrors,
won't stay still. Look the other way.
Behave as if she isn't there.
(The ghosts are building themselves a house,
only she is able to see inside it.)

The ghost's child
lands in the wings
of a fireplace. Burnt.
In a house full of *blue* sofas

(so the mother says). Is every house so blue,
so full of monograms—and crests—

                    and secrets?

She could be the white pillow in a fairy tale.

The shame they are making her feel,
letting it overflow with them
everywhere, all round the house—
Take this child, run away with her . . .

Was it to punish her
for being as wicked as *he* was?

They wanted to rob her of him,
so she would never, never know how he died.

Walk into the room and be ashamed.
Aunt Esther wanted her to know how he did
        crawling in a room   how he dead
she could not   never get   remember
unremember—How he died

He was rolling on the floor with his ulcers.

A coward by drink. Did they give him,
grant him anything? Did they give him
light talk, courtesy, did they give him a dollar?

It isn't pretty to extract these tales.

THE TROUBLE I HAVE IN HIGH PLACES

It could kick back, the gun—
it needed to be taught a lesson,
to stand in the closet with its back to us.
It had its own harsh moods
and drawbacks, like a rebellious daughter.

I was not to be counted on, was the lesson
I was learning; not normal. My words were bad,
and harmful to the natural sympathies of the world.
And I could be straightened out by a man, he said,
but who would do it, who would take me on?

I wouldn't say cheese, or have my cake and eat it too.
Mother stayed out of the discussion, in these cases.
What does it have to do with now, with the courage
to walk into high and dangerous places?

When as kids, he took us to the high places, windy and tall—
outside of buildings, up masts and the tallest trees;
was he teaching us to be like the masts of ships, to be
        like men,
or break our necks trying? Would it be foolish and
        womanly of me,
would it be normal, to look down and fall?

Coming-Out Party

He wanted to go to a dance long ago,
but decided to show up in his bedroom slippers.
The hostess was the debutante Brenda Frazier.
It was best to dress up, but he went there
showing off his broken-down bedroom slippers
and she was shocked. She had thought
he wanted to dance with her
but he was laughing   laughing

He had to run away then and there
to prove how forcefulness could win a war,
how he could set the styles, just like that!
He came out and ran the whole thing himself.

As he sang, and bragged about it,
it was warm. It was a warm summer night.
That sense of being in a cocoon:
a lazy, breezy, by-the-ocean feeling.

THE BEAR HE SHOT ON THEIR HONEYMOON IN MONTANA, THAT GROWLED, AND TRIED TO COME INTO THEIR TENT

This was home, and love and country:
him helping himself to another martini,
lighting the fire with a Cape Cod lighter,
with briquettes, with anything—
a pinecone, a rolled-up newspaper.

Each day he sang a new
honeymoon song of praise.
He tried helpfully growling,
he tried to come into the children's tents.
Without saying anything, without saying "briquettes"—
but whatever came into his head, he'd say it.

In the thickness of coat closets,
the hat racks, the gun racks.

Sitting down to dinner,
he reserved the choicest morsels
for himself. Look, look who he speared!
He was rearranging the food on their plates,
making them look away, tricking them for their dinners.
And look at all the white meat he speared!

THE SUNLIT BREAK

There is no sunlight
through these rooms,
no accent of purple flowers
against a stuccoed wall.

There are no lilies on the hilltop path just now.
The wind keeps opening a view
through a tall fuchsia hedge,
to a side room or sunroom,
an open, inviting space.

You can browse and be drawn
to that corner room
at the ocean side of the house.

A few crows fly from the treetops,
from nests wedged in the old hawthorns.

The sound of the wind
among the flowers
is the sound many years ago
along a shore road.

The cat is sleeping on his bed of grass.

You can see out through hinges,
thumb-size openings in the knotted trunks
of the rhododendron bushes.

Or feel your way past
a few late, crimson petals
down to the ocean of dark at the back of the house.

On the path which led from the house in Michigan
down to the lake, through a hedge.
Or the path which is now,
which you follow to the last detail.

PENTHOUSE

Our mother stood below, calling
Lee, Lee,
you're going to kill the children!

Below was a blur.
Cars turned the corner
of Madison and Seventy-ninth Street,
    waves speeding to a cliff.

I tried to ignore
    pent-up fear, his will
        for us to go higher, high above the terrace.

I could divide myself off from him—

                Catch her if she falls

I'm right here, Giny.   I'm below
to catch her if she falls   I'm normal
now, Giny.   Good signals.
The behavior of the signals was good.
Signals of the marriage were being exchanged.

Breath began to ripen
high on the terrace's tree.
Mother of fears, mother of rescues,
where are you now?

Calling, calling out below.
We were very young then,
Mother, we were tender and good.
Climbing the water tower on top of the building.
It became slow and difficult. We thought
clinging to the side of the building
was good. *Break me and my name now Mother?*
We thought crawling away from danger was good.

I go out, Mother of winds,
like the Navajo—who never fall.

Breath began to ripen in fear
high on the terrace,
above the thin wall of trees.

I go out, Mother of buildings,
crawling on a high ledge.
The beauty of fear was in it
for him, beautiful high tide of fear.
     As if the elevator took us up
then drew back and went away.

I go out onto the new day, Mother,
fighting the wind, like the Navajo—
but away from death.

HEARING THE VOICES

Reading the Vocal

THE MUSIC CABINET

Inside the room,
there is a music cabinet,
with handles of the evening curving down
into the silent, yellow-brown wood.
The iron handles are turning to rain,
to the heads of sea animals.

The thoughts of the yellow cabinet are in flames!
There are figures who gallop away into the darkness,
seated on dolphins, on bronze sea horses.

At a crossroads,
large creatures wait for us
to visit, and to bless them.

The great singing mothers
wait for us equally
to go up one by one,
and sing about beauty,
earthly love, and time.

They have set fire to the things of the earth!
They have set foot here, in this original room.

The sea horses
are at large; tragic
shapes invade the openness.

The hours are painted on the cabinet
in gold and in crystal letters.

And the great singing mothers
ask us to go with them,
into a forest of changeable vowels,
and of "O" sounds. The forest
of symbols, and oceanic beasts.

They know the seas are lonely, and are perfect,
that the sea horse has only one foot.

And they may ask us to release our voices
even among shadows; in shapes
calmed or caressed by the evening wind,
and in Forests of Weeping.

DELIA

When the child sat at the piano,
squeezing on the pedals, splashing,
Delia loved to sing!

Delia liked to see the windows
opening sky-blue, cranked by a slow,
elbow-bending effort.

"Believe me, if all those endearing young charms . . ."

She sang lustily,
she waltzed loud and breezy
in the forgotten room—

O believe me!

The windows sat, calm and window-seated.

The delightful windows were engaged.
They were opening like bouquets, white wedding
    bouquets—
Invitations! for those endearing young charms.

The windows sat peacefully, window-eyed.

And suddenly there was a voice,
the room was a rustle of chords,
and there'd be a crowd of homesick windows, opening!

DRIVEWAY

Ten o'clock in the morning.
Rain sank in each crevice.
The driveway sang,
under wheels of a descending Mercury.

The gravel voice poured,
as from a rainstick in Australia.
I stuck out my long neck like a giraffe—
And felt myself rebuild, within the water's voice.

Up to my knees
up to my waist
the driveway voice poured.

I felt myself descend
as down a ladder,
into a well. That voice with a *someday*
understood, and could take me in.

ELEPHANT

A green tent of vine leaves and ivy overhead.
The elephant carries the key
along a balustrade, above the garden.
He carries the sun key out-of-doors,
or sets it down on a table
in the sunroom.

The table opens:
birds like flying fish
carry Hope into the sunroom.

A table has eyes, tiger eyes like topaz
to follow the movements, the descent of nights
as they move out onto the terrace.
The elephant is a bell
that summons me.

I begin to know
William Blake
in the descent of nights,
begin to hear the accents
the familiar greetings—

The elephant, whose domain this is
carries the tray out
through long French doors.

My eyes search for the bearer of tidings,
for William Blake,
who followed the scent of wildflowers
into the ventriloquy of a house.

We step onto the staircase.
Noting the depths: fields carried
away by floods; the high-water marks on trees.

The elephant has sea-eyes
like a turtle, to follow the ancient
systems of knowledge.

                    We step out.
They move away, as if over a dance floor,
and are lost to us.

A wishbone is wishing for the growth
of new life into these rooms.

And now the house opens.
The elephant, whose back I rode on as a child,
carries evening out onto the terrace.

He carries vines up the walk,
so the pavements will be vine-shadowed.

He places a small drink at the grandmother's elbow.
It is evening by the grandfather clock
on the landing. By firelight and lamplight.

Evening has come. He carries evening
on a tray through the long French doors.

HEARING THE VOICES

Hearing the voices of birds
in a clearing,
as if in a calmer, more crystal world:
keeping to itself in the woods.

She lingered,
then quickly opened the side gate.

As if opening a book
that led out into the woods:
on a trail past the greenhouse,
flowerpots, a kitchen garden.

Who planted these paths?
One half went whispering
past sheds and a garden;
the other path circled a round hill
planted with pines,
where the light barely penetrated.

Pine needles underfoot, the odor of mushrooms.
The mysterious pinewoods knitted
to a pine-cushion, or pincushion.

Here you were scared
you possibly scared away the rabbit

that was hiding behind bushes
in a hole near the greenhouse steps.

She would go where nothing mattered
and everything mattered—
nothing was held back
or wasted.

The smooth hymns of the pine needles
cushioned her footsteps.

They gave her gooseflesh—

the goose-girl
hearing her voices
among the cabbages and leeks.

She would go deeper into the woods,
away from the world, whenever time allowed.

Deer circled the clearing.
They passed by, not seeing her
as she knelt like Joan of Arc.

Listening to wind high above in the pines;
hearing the a cappella voices:
birdsong and the ripples of a stream.

Voices eavesdropped:
she would go with them gladly.

She would go to great lengths
to find her voices later   after the war.

The pines appear and disappear—
they know her. Pines grow
at her doorstep
this beautiful morning.
Over the pine needles like silk
is the finest place to walk.

GOATS CLIMB THE DIVIDE

They were sewing,
butting their heads through canvas
to sew the maroon and green heather,
the bright canvas waves.

I liked the way they climbed
into the rough sky above hills
with ribbed houses of coral—
the blue and white shreds
of beaded clouds.

The goats looked down at me once,
curling their way over hills.
They were walking through the oval night.

They worked their way under the wire
then out, through a torn, iron gate.

They climbed the nervous corners
of the divide, to go on upward.
Keeping the outline of a path
through rough seas of heather;
finding a foothold in bare rock.

I liked the way the goats
climbed the divide of hills.

They were singing in their hides
to sew the few, bright curves of heather,
the maroon and green waves.

ALONG THE QUARRY ROAD

The Uncle Who Believed in Mountains

He kept turning up in the hall at midnight, straight from the war. On a mission for the OSS, they parachuted high into the mountains.

They were snowbound, waiting for the Sherpa guides. Tallow candles reflected upward on high cheekbones. Moving back and forth between tents, they carried skins of wine and clarified butter. In the high moonlight, the magnet of mountains, they seemed to be indifferent to their conditions. Will they come home frostbitten, and will they cry out at night? The child doesn't know. They stay up late that night, trading the stories back and forth.

War kept them so far from home. Among the ravines with the guide, with different guides. Each has a strength that can pull you through the night. Will they lose fingers and toes and will they come home lame? The child doesn't know. Up ahead they are growing snow-blind with their guides: Childhood and Early Sorrow. The guides could run up a mountain straight, without being tired. Within the penthouse on the 12th or 13th—or no, the 14th—floor their eyes have grown younger and more talkative. Comfort of the small Mongolian horses, slipping past and escaping north into China, to Chiang Kai-shek.

GEOGRAPHY LESSON

She learned the names of rivers
and of mountain ranges.
For rooms full of visitors. So willing was she—
it was a way to impress the new men in her family,
who were on leave from the Pacific
or Pearl Harbor, facing a long, silent war.

Always maps, and the nervous
mapmakers, changing their minds.

She learned to follow
the slow curves of a river
to a source in the high wall
of the Andes. To follow
the Orinoco, the Amazon, the Nile.

Sometimes the rivers went underground.
You could hear them murmur the names
through canyons and grottoes,
emerging up ahead.

Always the maps, big glistening maps
with worn-out folds,
which Time was always changing.
The blue and brown and green fields
asked to borrow a new history—
changing names, or having their names erased.

Her own name had been changed—
the forever name buried,
left at the border.

She could unfold the maps completely
and follow the drift, as if allowed to swim away
from the family boat,
where they were sitting out on deck,
heads down over nautical charts—
at some distance.

Slow curves in a northerly direction,
to the high points, where the mountains become one.
Does this ever happen?

To My Achill Neighbors
in the Wind and Rain

First I'll call the sheep
from the rivers to the sun.
They lift themselves across the road.

Sheep: a riptide,
a breaking through, belonging.

Like finding my own tongue.

How to be there, building with them.
The sun along a promontory,
beating down. I'll skim through,
taking my time,
be sheer along these cliffs.

Like the gannet, turning in space,
the shearwater and fulmar.

The cliffs themselves,
turning:
how they eat into the day.

Bring the Lambs

Lambs climbed down
Over walls of the lambing shed.

They awoke inside a fence—

(All this was taking place *inside*
I was finding my lost breath
the sea-wind   the lambs)

Their small lives expanding
allowed time to open and pass through a world.

I awoke in the ruby
of their wayward sounds;
the head-down, washed-out
sky of sounds.

Lambs climbed down,
let walls and fences wander
through peaceful woods and across farmlands.

Their washed-out, shaky sounds
played with the lichen of stone walls.

They exploded over walls, down roads—
like a flower episode; a flower hidden
inside a seed—

telling roads to wander and flicker out.

They climbed over the bones
of people and brooks.

Something in me melted
to remember these sounds.
They took the breath of dawn with them,
climbing through woods.

The sheep, the lambs came running to me
out of the open pen of the years.

RIDDLE

What was it the child heard in the different voices of the house, that was inside clocks, in the stillness of the walnut cabinets? It was intricate as a church bazaar, but could be fitted inside a walnut. It was in the crystal smelling-salts bottle, held beneath her grandmother's nose when she was feeling faint; in the drop of brown medicine taken on a spoon, in a sugar cube.

The sun moved like a dancer across the still design of the Persian carpet. It was in the body of the world, that "Pride of the Flesh" her grandmother spoke of, when she described the singers she had known: the way they sounded, the way they moved. It was in the bodies of women.

Perhaps it was that "Mother-of-Pearl" they sometimes spoke of: the beauty of the world, formed out of "Mother-of-Pearl," that smilingly or obligingly held itself under their noses night and day, and was great and many-sided as a wedding cake, but could be fitted inside a kiss.

DEATH

Death could come among them, speaking Latin. With a formal bow, he might lay his wager at the front door. He might buy them a shell necklace, or an ice cream cone. Death could come calling, be admitted to the spacious dark of the downstairs hallway, or a small, indoors garden room. Was he bunched into the shadow that was always near them?

Death was a stiff old gentleman. In his own house, he might lay a bet with you, that you could not identify the animal on the hand-painted dining room wallpaper. If you won, if you had guessed it right, you'd have to give the money to your favorite charity. Death was Mr. Henry Costa.

Or it was her grandmother's mother, leaning from the mantel in an ivory satin dress. Reading late one night on the living room sofa she said, "Kiss me, William, I'm dying," and she did. Death was her great-grandmother, in a satin gown.

Along the Quarry Road

The grass hummocks are like pillows
where I lay my head down,
hear the green calls of lambs
around me on the hillside.

This stone house: a cradle,
balanced on green hill-waves.

Pretensions of the wind
    to steal it all away:
the cloud, pillow, rooftop, house wall.

I plunge, I follow the sheep
uphill. The road meanders,
pulling me away from house and boundary line,
the settled life of the fields.

The mountain descends
behind a hill. Wind drops,
the sun comes out as I emerge
on high ground, the dazzling white heaps
of the quarry embankments.

Climb past the sleeping quarry.
Sliding heaps of white slag,

ghostly slag. Here the road is broken.
Choked with erosion, with the quarry's broad white stones,
it begins to disappear among the gullies.

Glamour of mountains,
     the cloud-swept home of wild goats and sheep;
and living contours of the rock:

the great curves,
     with slopes between, where nobody comes;
gently curving descents
with soft-spoken accents:
     Slievemore . . . Accorymore . . . Croaghan.

Places without addresses,
     that blend into one another
in the morning light;
districts of nomad shadows and a few black crows.

You could fall down a cliff
in the dark, if you were lost here.
There are no boundaries, no markers,
and you must trust to your instinct
to get across to the other side.

The stones stand at odd angles
from the roadbed, like a cradle
landlocked, motionless in the fields.
Or a road that has widened, with a stream
through the middle—until it disappears,
quietly, into the fields on either hand.

LIKE MUSIC

I had to close my eyes
as I came downhill.
I didn't bring anything with me.

Sheep went circling,
lambs tumbled over a wall.
Their seaward faces,
small mouths opening.

I had tree-sounds,
I was a salamander, a grey cloud.
What happened to me then,
when hillsides poured, the tree trunks opened?

The alphabet was lifting,
letting our thoughts open and pass through:
wind through an orchard,
or lambs above, on a green headland.

When we stepped across a threshold
they were lying on straw
in the corner, like heaped-up rags.
Just born, and they began to sing.

Lambs wandered up and down the roads
like music. They stepped across hillsides
under a fern-wall, looked inside a hedge.

Talking to each other,
keeping in touch with the ewes on the hill.

Last night I awoke.
I was finding a tree trunk
to sleep inside. Bark of the willow,
the pin oak, the sycamore.

I was looking for lost tree bark.
First the tough integument,
then a closer, *inside* bark
like the skin of an almond.

The alphabet was shrinking,
earth was shrinking away from us.

I had to sink way down,
remember the contours of each note.
Feeling my way along ditch banks and rivers.

I was keeping in touch
with zero, like the lambs.
I had trusted them with my grief,
and they spoke to me:

through the inside walls of childhood
and above, on a green headland.